Hetty's 100 HATS

Story by Janet Slingsby

Illustrated by Emma Dodd

Good  Books

Intercourse, PA 17534
800/762-7171
www.goodbks.com

Hetty had three hats.
A yellow straw hat to wear on hot, sunny days.

A blue waterproof hat
to wear on rainy days.

And a red woolly hat
to keep her ears warm
on cold winter days.

Hetty liked her hats. And so she was very pleased when her brother Henry's head got too big for his green baseball cap.

"Can I have that hat, please?" Hetty asked. Her brother happily handed it over.

A few days later, Hetty was invited to her cousin Peter's birthday party at the Pizza Palace. She brought home her pink party hat and wore it nonstop for three days.

Hetty's father said, "That reminds me, Hetty. I am going to buy you a hard hat to wear when you go out riding on your scooter."

Hetty happily counted her hats.
"One, two, three, four, five, six!"

The next day Hetty went to see her grandma. Hetty told her all about her six hats and Hetty's grandma said, "Look in the attic. I think you will find some more hats up there."

And Hetty found four hats.

"That one belonged to my Great Aunt Jemima."

"That's Grandpa's old gardening hat."

"I think that was your great, great grandmother's very best Sunday hat."

"And that is the hat I was wearing when I met your grandpa for the very first time."

Hetty's grandma said she could take all the hats home with her.

"Ten hats!" said Hetty's mom. "Have you got enough hats now, Hetty?"

"Oh no!" said Hetty. "I'd like to have lots more. In fact, I would like to have one hundred hats!" Hetty wasn't sure how many one hundred was, but she thought it sounded very important.

"That is a lot of hats, Hetty," her mother said. "Perhaps you should aim for thirty. Thirty hats would be a big collection."

"One hundred!" said Hetty in a very determined voice. And she immediately started her search for things to put on her head. In no time at all, Hetty had found fourteen extraordinary household hats.

When Hetty's auntie came to see her, she was surprised to see Hetty wearing a colander. Hetty explained that she was creating a collection of one hundred hats.

"Well, I have come to ask you to be my bridesmaid," said Hetty's aunt. "Yes please," said Hetty.

So her auntie took Hetty to meet the designer who was making her wedding dress. And he gave Hetty five fashionable hats left over from his Spring show.

Hetty looked lovely in her bridesmaid's outfit.
And she wore a wonderful circle of silk flowers on her head.

"Thirty hats," Hetty muttered to herself
as the photographer took her picture.

Everyone at the wedding was feeling happy and generous, so when Hetty asked them if they happened, by any chance, to have any spare hats, lots of people promised to find hats for her. Next day emails flew around the world. PLEASE SEND HATS TO HETTY was the message.

And soon parcels covered in strange and exotic stamps began to arrive at Hetty's house. In all, there were twenty exciting hats!

"I've brought you lots of exciting looking parcels this week," the postman said to Hetty. "May I ask what's inside them all?"

"Hats!" said Hetty. "I've got fifty but I need lots, lots more."
So the postman told the people in Hetty's town that he knew a little girl who was just crazy about hats. And next time Hetty went into town . . .

Bob at the building site gave her a hard hat.

Mr. Cook at the restaurant gave her a chef's hat and a waitress's cap.

Mrs. Needles at the sewing shop gave her a hat knitted from bright colored pieces of wool.

Mrs. Saddler at the riding school gave her an old riding hat and a jockey's colorful cap.

The lady at the toy shop gave her a witch's hat left over from Halloween.

Fred at the fire station presented her with a fire helmet.

And the ladies and gentlemen
at the retirement home gave her
six hats and told her wonderful
stories to go with them.
The nurse gave her a
spare nurse's cap, too.

Hetty counted her hats. She had $sixty$-$five$ now.

Days went by and no more hats appeared.

Hetty began to think she would never find $thirty$-$five$ more hats to complete her collection.

She even went out on windy days in the hope that a hat or two might blow her way. But none did.

Hetty's teacher wondered why Hetty wasn't listening in class. "I am thinking about hats," said Hetty. "Hetty, do pay attention," said her teacher. "We are talking about the class history project. What do you think we should do for the parents' evening next week?"

"Have a hat parade!" said Hetty. And the whole class made and brought in historical hats. "A great effort," said Hetty's teacher after the parade. "But I don't know where I can store twenty-one hats." "I don't mind taking them home with me," said Hetty.

Hetty's friend Susan asked her how many hats she had now.

"Eighty-six!" Hetty said proudly. "It's my birthday next week and you are all invited to my hat-making party. I want to complete the collection on my birthday!"

"How many more do you need?" asked Tom. Hetty thought hard.

"Thirteen," she said. "Then I will have one hundred hats."

That Saturday, Hetty collected a huge pile of paper, card, ribbon, string, bits of fabric, old birthday cards, felt pens, scissors, crayons, and sticky tape.

She helped her mother cover the table with an old blanket and she set out pots of glue and packets of pins.

Hetty and her friends worked hard all afternoon. They managed to finish ten exclusive, original handmade hats.

"Three more!" muttered Hetty worriedly as she waved goodbye to her friends.

"Cheer up, Hetty!" said her mom. "I've got some more birthday presents for you."

There was an old bonnet that Hetty's grandma had found, a sparkly pink beret from Hetty's auntie, a wonderful beach hat from her mom and dad, and a birthday letter from her brother away at camp.

"Your collection is complete now, Hetty," said her mother in a very pleased voice. Hetty hurried off to put the new hats in her bedroom with the rest of her hat collection.

MY 100 HAT COLLECTION

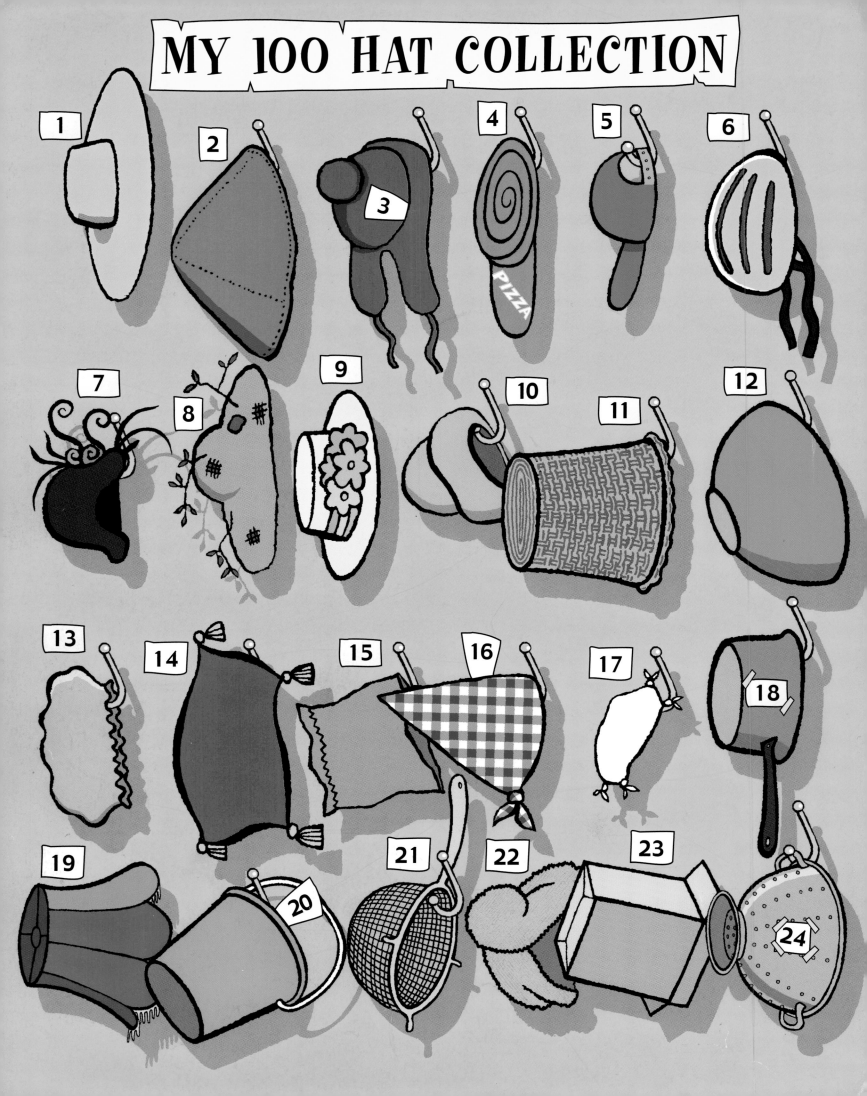

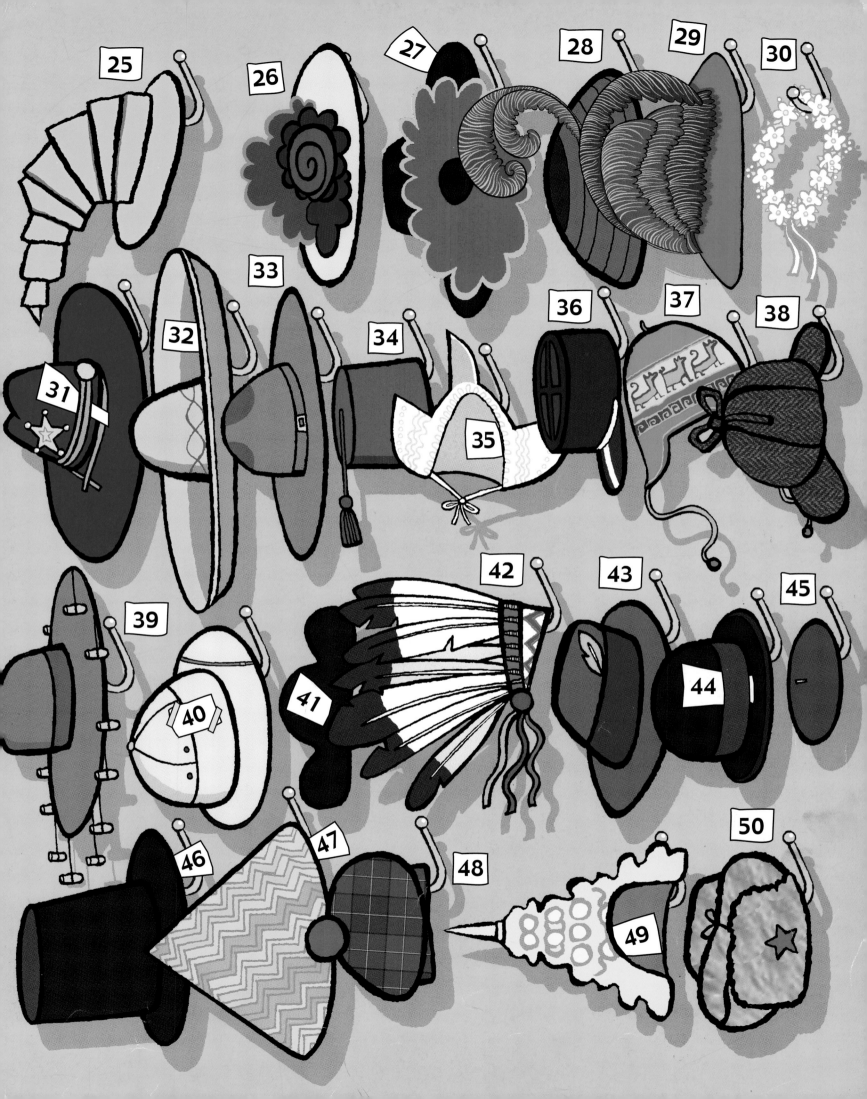

85

86

87

88

89

90

91

92

93

94

95

96

97

98

99

100

"Oh no!" said Hetty. "I've only got ninety-nine hats. I need one more hat!" And Hetty was so upset that she cried, even though it was her birthday.

Hetty's mother tried to cheer her up. "We can make another hat together."

"We can't," sobbed Hetty. "We've used up all the hat-making bits and I did so want to finish my collection today."

"Look," said Hetty's mom. "You haven't read Henry's letter."

"It's not a hat!" said Hetty sadly. But she opened the letter and this is what she found inside.

Dear Hetty,

Sorry I didn't get you a hat for your birthday. Here is an emergency hat-making pattern in case you need an extra hat in a hurry. You only need a piece of newspaper to make it.

Happy Birthday!

love,

Henry

How to Make a Newspaper Hat

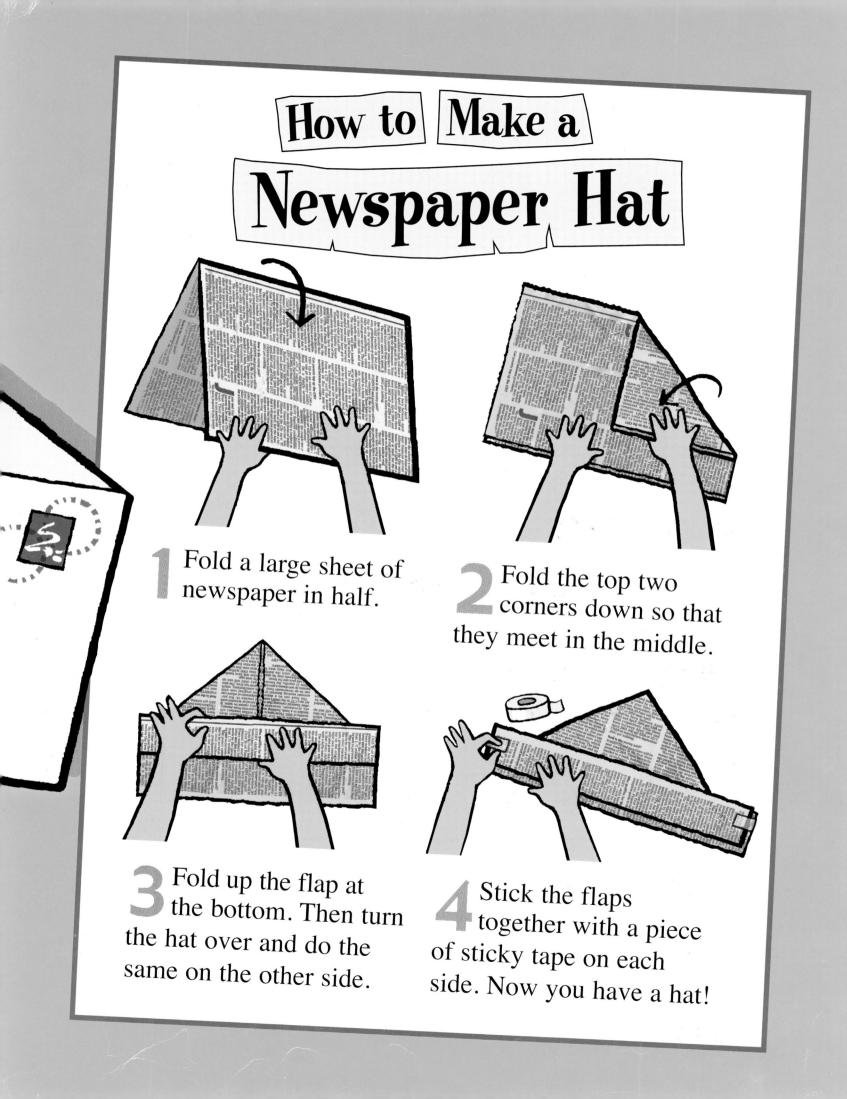

1 Fold a large sheet of newspaper in half.

2 Fold the top two corners down so that they meet in the middle.

3 Fold up the flap at the bottom. Then turn the hat over and do the same on the other side.

4 Stick the flaps together with a piece of sticky tape on each side. Now you have a hat!

As she twirled around, showing off her newspaper hat, Hetty caught sight of her mother's new pink shoes.

"I like *shoes*," said Hetty thoughtfully.